Dear Parent:

Your child's love of reading starts here!

Every child learns to read in a different way and at his or her own speed. Some go back and forth between reading levels and read favorite books again and again. Others read through each level in order. You can help your young reader improve and become more confident by encouraging his or her own interests and abilities. From books your child reads with you to the first books he or she reads alone, there are I Can Read Books for every stage of reading:

SHARED READING
Basic language, word repetition, and whimsical illustrations, ideal for sharing with your emergent reader

BEGINNING READING
Short sentences, familiar words, and simple concepts for children eager to read on their own

READING WITH HELP
Engaging stories, longer sentences, and language play for developing readers

READING ALONE
Complex plots, challenging vocabulary, and high-interest topics for the independent reader

I Can Read Books have introduced children to the joy of reading since 1957. Featuring award-winning authors and illustrators and a fabulous cast of beloved characters, I Can Read Books set the standard for beginning readers.

A lifetime of discovery begins with the magical words "I Can Read!"

Visit www.icanread.com for information
on enriching your child's reading experience.

I Can Read® and I Can Read Book® are trademarks of HarperCollins Publishers.

Pete the Cat: Super Pete
Text copyright © 2020 by Kimberly and James Dean
Illustrations copyright © 2020 by James Dean
Pete the Cat is a registered trademark of Pete the Cat, LLC.
All rights reserved. Manufactured in China.

Library of Congress Control Number: 2019956253
ISBN 978-0-06-286853-4 (trade bdg.) —ISBN 978-0-06-286850-3 (pbk.)

Book design by Chrisila Maida

20 21 22 23 24 LSC 10 9 8 7 6 5 4 3 2 1   ❖   First Edition

Pete the Cat

SUPER PETE

by Kimberly & James Dean

HARPER

An Imprint of HarperCollins Publishers

Pete the Cat is out for a walk.

Pete listens to the owls.

He listens to the frogs.

Just then, Pete hears a beep.

It is not coming from outside.

It is coming from his watch!

Pete races home.

It is time for Pete the Cat

to become Super Pete!

Pete presses a button in his room.

The wall slides away.

Pete sees a set of steps.

Down, down, down he goes.

Pete steps into his lair.
It is full of groovy things
to help him fight crime.

MOST
WANTED

RIME
OMPUTER

Pete the Cat puts on

his awesome cat suit.

He puts on his cape

and his sneakers.

Now Super Pete is ready

to save the city.

Pete sees a flashing light.

There is a message

on his computer.

It is the mayor!

"Come quick, Super Pete,"

the mayor says.

"We need your help.

There is trouble at the warehouse."

Pete pulls a lever.

Whoosh!

Pete's nifty jet

sinks into his lair.

Pete hops into the jet.

He zips into the air.

Super Pete is on his way

to save the day!

Pete races through the sky.

He hits a button.

The jet shimmers.

The jet disappears.

Now the jet is invisible.

No one will know
Super Pete is coming.

Pete hovers over the warehouse.

He straps on a parachute.

He jumps.

Pete lands on the roof.

He goes inside the warehouse.

It is dark.

He cannot see.

Pete puts on his

night vision goggles.

He sees two bad guys.

They are carrying a box.

Pete picks up a rock.

He puts it in his slingshot.

The rock hits the box.

The bad guys drop the box.

They climb out a window!

Pete races to the window.

The bad guys have a boat.

They are getting away!

Pete pushes a button

on his cat suit.

His sneakers turn to flippers.

A mask closes over his face.

Pete jumps into the water.

He swims after the bad guys.

Pete takes a rope

from his pocket.

He twirls it over his head.

Pete aims.

He throws.

The rope catches the boat.

Pete pulls himself

along the rope.

Pete climbs into

the bad guys' boat.

He ties up the bad guys.

Pete pushes a button

on his watch.

His jet appears above him.

Pete pulls the bad guys

into his jet.

Pete brings the bad guys

to the mayor.

Super Pete saved the day!